THE HALLOWEEN HOAX

by Bonnie West • pictures by Patt Blumer

CAROLRHODA BOOKS

MINNEAPOLIS, MINNESOTA U.S.A.

To my family

International Standard Book Number: 0-87614-173-4
Library of Congress Catalog Card Number: 81-68853

1 2 3 4 5 6 7 8 9 10 87 86 85 84 83 82

A
CAROLRHODA
MINI-
MYSTERY

"Look! Up on the stairs! It's a bird. It's a plane. No, it's Superman and his powerful companion Wonder Woman!"

Jane and Eddy were standing at the top of the stairs. They had just put their coats on Geri's bed. They looked down at their friend Phil, who had made the announcement. He was dressed as a clown.

"Hey, Phil," said Eddy. "Look at these legs! No stuffing needed here. Must be all the running we do." Eddy struck a Superman pose. He stuck out his chest. It was full of padding that he had sewn into his costume. They all laughed.

"Those are great costumes," said Lydia. She was dressed as a magician. "Too bad Phil doesn't have one this year." She smiled and tapped Phil's arm with her white-tipped magic wand.

"Very funny, Lydia," said Phil.

"That's a great costume you have on, Lydia," Jane said. "The wand and the magic hat are perfect. I can't wait to see your magic show."

They all went into the living room. There were eight other kids at the party. Little Red Riding Hood, a pirate, and a fat ballerina were talking to Mr. Bane by the fireplace. Mr. Bane had on a costume too. Most of the kids knew him as one of the teachers at school. But tonight he was just Geri's father. And this was Geri's party.

"Hi, Mr. Bane," said Eddy. "Who are you? A Russian soldier?"

Mr. Bane smiled. "I guess history will never be as much fun as goofing off, will it, Eddy? I'm Napolean. And he would have hated to hear you call him a Russian!"

Just then Geri walked into the room. "Is everyone ready for the magic show?" she asked.

"We sure are," said Jane. "But where's Lydia?"

Suddenly Lydia rushed through the hall into the living room. "Oh, forgive me, forgive me!" she said. "I didn't mean to be late for my own magic show." Lydia ran to the front of the room.

"I was just outside thinking about my magic tricks, looking for shooting stars, listening to the crickets, and brrrr, getting much too cold. But please, sit down, sit down. And everyone watch carefully!" Lydia pulled a stream of scarves out of her magic hat.

"Boy, is she dramatic," Eddy whispered to Jane. "I bet she was late on purpose."

"I don't think so," replied Jane. "She seemed nervous about something. And there was something wrong with what she said."

"I know, I know," said Eddy. "The sky is cloudy. So she couldn't have been looking for shooting stars, right? I know you and your detective mind. You're just looking for a mystery to solve. You should have come as Sherlock Holmes instead of Wonder Woman!"

"That's not it, Eddy. Oh, never mind. It's probably nothing." Jane looked around the room. "Where did Phil go?" she asked.

"He left when Lydia came in," answered Eddy. "He didn't feel well, so he went to lie down. Now let's watch the show. Lydia is pretty good."

Lydia did all kinds of tricks. She made
things disappear by tapping them with her
wand. She did some card tricks. And she
talked non-stop during the whole show.

Everyone stood up and clapped at the
end of the magic show. "Bravo, Lydia!"
cried Eddy. Lydia took a bow and started
gathering her props together.

"Let's go into the dining room," said Geri. "There's lots of food in there."

Just then Mr. Bane walked into the room. "Wait a minute, kids," he said. "Before anyone goes anywhere, I want to talk to you. Let's go into the den."

Mr. Bane walked down the hall. The kids all followed close behind. Phil was coming out of the bathroom just as everyone went into the den. He followed them inside.

"What's going on?" Phil asked Eddy.

"I don't know," Eddy answered. "What's that?" He pointed to a small white cap on the end of Phil's finger.

"This? I'm not sure. I came in here to lie down and saw it on the floor. I figured it was a Chap-Stick cap. Mr. Bane probably has a melting mess in one of his pockets."

"Quiet please," said Mr. Bane. "This is serious. I had a ten dollar bill lying on my desk in here and now it's gone. One of you must have taken it since no one else has been in the house tonight."

"Well, I know who took it," Lydia spoke up loudly. "He did." She pointed at Phil. He looked pale and very surprised.

"I know he took it because I saw him coming out of this room during my magic show," Lydia said. "None of you could see him. I wondered what was so important that he couldn't watch my show. And now I know."

Jane and Eddy could hardly believe their ears. Everyone turned and looked at Phil.

"Is that true, Phil? Were you in here?" asked Mr. Bane.

"Yes," said Phil. "But I didn't steal your money. I didn't feel well, so I came in here to lie down. Then I went into the bathroom for a drink of water. I came out just as everyone was coming in here. I really didn't take it, Mr. Bane."

"It sounds to me like you did, Phil," Lydia said.

"I don't think so, Lydia," said Jane. "And I think I can prove that what he said is true. Look at Phil's cheek. There's a big smear on it. There's also a smear on the couch over there. Phil's only crime was

getting clown make-up on the couch. No thief would lie down for a rest at the scene of the crime. But you seem pretty anxious to blame him, Lydia. Is it to cover up for yourself?"

"What?" cried Lydia. "I couldn't have taken it. I was doing the magic show."

"Who said it was taken *during* the magic show?" Jane said. "When you said you'd been listening to the crickets earlier, I thought you might be lying. Crickets don't chirp when it's below 55 degrees outside. And you couldn't have been looking for shooting stars because it's cloudy."

"I was just chattering when I said that," replied Lydia. "It doesn't prove that I wasn't outside. And you can't prove I was ever in this room."

"But I can!" said Eddy. He reached over and took the small white cap from Phil. "It doesn't take a magician to figure out where the money is, either. This cap is from the end of your magic wand. I noticed during the show that your wand looked different than it had earlier. It's because there wasn't a cap on the end. You stole the money, Lydia. You rolled it up and stuck it in your wand. But you didn't put the cap back on tight enough and it fell off."

Lydia's face turned red. She looked down at the floor. Mr. Bane looked inside Lydia's wand and found the money.

"I'm afraid I'll have to call your parents,
Lydia," he said. "The rest of you kids can
go get something to eat."

Eddy, Jane, and Phil walked into the dining room together.

"It's lucky both of you were here," said Phil. "I don't know how I could have proved that I didn't take that money."

"It was nothing, Phil." Jane grinned. "Not for Wonder Woman and Superman!"